SPECIAL MESSAGE TO READERS

This book is published under the auspices of

THE ULVERSCROFT FOUNDATION

(registered charity No. 264873 UK)

Established in 1972 to provide funds for research, diagnosis and treatment of eye diseases. Examples of contributions made are: —

A Children's Assessment Unit at Moorfield's Hospital, London.

•

Twin operating theatres at the Western Ophthalmic Hospital, London.

•

A Chair of Ophthalmology at the Royal Australian College of Ophthalmologists.

•

The Ulverscroft Children's Eye Unit at the Great Ormond Street Hospital For Sick Children, London.

You can help further the work of the Foundation by making a donation or leaving a legacy. Every contribution, no matter how small, is received with gratitude. Please write for details to:

THE ULVERSCROFT FOUNDATION,
The Green, Bradgate Road, Anstey,
Leicester LE7 7FU, England.
Telephone: (0116) 236 4325

In Australia write to:

THE ULVERSCROFT FOUNDATION,
c/o The Royal Australian and New Zealand
College of Ophthalmologists,
94-98 Chalmers Street, Surry Hills,
N.S.W. 2010, Australia

NEVER LET GO

Tom Lockey should be on a beach holiday with his son, but his ex-wife suddenly cancels, saying Josh is ill. When Josh and his bike go missing, Tom frantically scours the Dorset coastline in case Josh has decided to come alone. Rowena Jackson is also on holiday with her daughter, Amy, who sees visions of a boy with a mark on his face . . . Tom and Rowena draw closer together as they try to find Josh before it's too late.

DELLA GALTON

NEVER LET GO

Complete and Unabridged

LINFORD
Leicester

First published in Great Britain in 2003

First Linford Edition
published 2011

British Library CIP Data

Galton, Della.
Never let go.- -(Linford romance library)
1. Divorced men- - Family relationships- -
Fiction. 2. Missing children- -England- -
Dorset- - Fiction. 3. Mothers and daughters- -
Fiction. 4. Romantic suspense novels.
5. Large type books.
I. Title II. Series
823.9′2–dc22

ISBN 978–1–4448–0795–0

Published by
F. A. Thorpe (Publishing)
Anstey, Leicestershire

Set by Words & Graphics Ltd.
Anstey, Leicestershire
Printed and bound in Great Britain by
T. J. International Ltd., Padstow, Cornwall

This book is printed on acid-free paper

1

He couldn't shake off the feeling that he was being watched. He stopped sketching and, twisting round on his chair, shielded his eyes against the sun. Once again, he could see no one. Behind him sand dunes, stringy with grass, undulated back up towards the cliffs. In front of him, sand the colour of digestive biscuits sloped towards the glittering sea. Maybe the heat was getting to him, he thought. He'd been out since half-past nine.

The beach itself was dotted with families, which was why he'd sat up here, out of the way. He didn't want to be reminded that he was no longer part of a family. That he would have to watch his son growing up in weekend chunks — and that was when Susannah was in a generous mood.

He'd just turned back to the easel

and picked up his pencil again, when a small voice said, 'Are you drawing the beach?'

He jumped, glancing about.

'Over here,' the voice said, and he swivelled round. A head appeared from behind the biggest of the sand dunes. Curly hair and huge brown eyes. She was wearing a red tie-up bikini. She couldn't have been much more than seven, he judged, but there was something in her expression that was older. Then she arched her eyebrows and he decided he was imagining things.

'Well, are you drawing it, then?'

'Yes,' he said. 'I am.'

'You haven't done much. I've been watching you for ages.'

So he hadn't been going mad.

Without saying anything else, she climbed over the sand dune and scrambled across to him.

'Where's your mummy?' he said automatically.

'Asleep. What's your name?'

'Tom.'

'I'm Amy. Can I see your picture?'

'I thought you'd already seen it.'

'Not closer, I haven't. Can you lift me up?'

Lifting her up was out of the question, Tom decided. Surely her mother couldn't really be asleep? He stood up and scanned the beach. There were no likely prospects in sight, but if someone were in the dip of the next sand dune along, you wouldn't see them.

'My mummy won't mind,' Amy said, putting her head on one side and reminding him of a sparrow. 'Your shoulders are red. You need to put some more lotion on.'

He smiled at her. 'I never burn,' he said, which was true normally. Susannah had always been envious of his olive skin, which only turned a deeper colour in the sun. 'I think we'd better go and find your mummy, Amy. You shouldn't really go wandering off, you know. She'll be worried.'

'OK.'

She took his hand and he felt suddenly annoyed with this unknown mother who seemed oblivious to her child's whereabouts.

'She's over here,' Amy said, letting go of his hand and skipping away from him — but he decided to go with her, just to be sure.

As they approached a row of sand dunes, he saw a woman stand up and shield her eyes from the sun, her face anxious. He followed Amy cautiously and, as they got closer, he had an impression of longish, dark hair, a slight figure — and something more worrying. The woman was swaying slightly. He paused and the woman turned in their direction.

'Amy! Where have you been, you naughty . . . ?' She broke off, saw him and didn't look pleased. 'How many . . . times have I said . . . ?'

She put a hand up to her face and Amy turned to him, raised her eyebrows and said, 'Oh dear, Mummy's gone all blurry again.'

Tom could feel a little pit of coldness inside him. The woman was obviously drunk. She couldn't even get her words out and she looked as though she might fall over at any moment. Caught between concern for Amy and a desire to tell her mother exactly what he thought about such irresponsible behaviour, he hesitated.

'It's all right, Tom,' Amy said, giving him a look that told him this sort of thing happened all the time. 'Mummy's . . .'

But before she could finish her sentence, the woman suddenly sat down heavily on the dunes and Amy, spurred into action, ran across to her side.

Tom took a hesitant step towards where she sat.

'Go away,' she said and there was a look in her dark eyes that dared him to argue.

'But I — '

'Didn't you hear me? We're fine.' She was making an enormous effort to get her words out and he backed away, shocked. Maybe he ought to tell someone, but it wasn't the sort of beach where lifeguards patrolled. The best thing he could do, he decided, was to go back to his easel and keep an eye on them. If anything happened to that little girl, he wouldn't be able to forgive himself.

'Bye-bye, Tom,' Amy said.

'Bye,' he said, turning away from them and walking back to his easel and chair. All thoughts of sketching had gone from his mind now, so he just sat down, appalled. For the first time in a long while, he found himself wishing Susannah were here. Amy's mother would have reacted differently to a woman, he was sure. She wouldn't have seen her as a threat. Even if he'd had Josh with him, he might have got on better. He'd have been able to talk to her, parent to parent.

He felt a wave of bitter despair. Josh would have been with him if Susannah hadn't been messing him around again. This holiday was supposed to have been for him and his son, but at the last minute Susannah had said that Josh wasn't feeling too well and it would be better if she kept him at home. Whether this was true or not, Tom didn't know. Josh often seemed to be ill when it was his turn to have him. He'd gone along with it so far because he didn't want to risk alienating himself even further from his ex-wife and jeopardising his access to Josh. Susannah never said he couldn't see his son, but getting her to honour the arrangements they'd made was a different matter.

He rubbed his shoulders distractedly. They were starting to get a bit sore. Amy had been right after all. Pulling on a T-shirt, he glanced across to the sand dune and saw that her mother was standing up now and appeared to be packing things into a canvas rucksack. A short while later, he saw her and Amy walking up the beach, hand in hand. To his relief, she was walking perfectly steadily.

About half an hour after they'd left, he went too. Back to the holiday caravan park on the cliff top. He showered in the tiny cubicle, pulled on some clean shorts, sat on the uncomfortable bench seating that ran around the lounge area of the van, and looked out at the panoramic view across the bay. This would have been the perfect holiday for him and Josh, but he hadn't a clue what he was going to do here for a week on his own. A single man in a holiday park full of families. He was probably better off forgetting the whole thing and driving back home. At least there he could bury himself in his work and finish the series of illustrations he was doing for a Christmas card manufacturer. He hadn't brought much in the way of painting stuff with him, just some bits and pieces to sketch with that he'd put in at the last minute when Susannah had phoned and told him Josh wasn't going to be able to come.

'Do you think he'll be better tomorrow?' he'd asked her guardedly. 'I could wait and drive down in the morning. It seems a shame to disappoint him when he's been looking forward to it.'

'It's not my fault he's ill, Tom.' Her voice had been sharp. 'I'm not keeping him at home for nothing, you know.'

'Of course not.'

'You go on your holiday. It'd be silly to waste your money.'

'Seems a bit pointless on my own.'

She'd sighed. 'Look, I'll tell you what I'll do. If he's better in the next couple of days, I'll drop him off myself. It's near Mum's, so we could call in and see her on the way. Kill two birds with one stone. I can't say fairer than that.'

He'd given her the address of the site and the number of the van, though she had his mobile phone number anyway. With hindsight, that was probably what she'd wanted all along. Susannah liked to be in control of things. She was chronically insecure and he'd found out not long into their marriage that she was only happy if she knew the ins and outs of everything he was doing. Even now that they were separated, she liked to know what was going on, hooking details of his life from him as a fisherman hooks fish from a river. He knew she cross-examined Josh too, which made him uneasy, but there was little he could do about it. He'd phone her later and see how Josh was. Even if he only came for the tail end of the week, it would be worthwhile staying on.

He glanced at his watch. Just before six and definitely time for a meal. Breakfast in the campsite café seemed a long time ago and it had been too hot to eat on the beach. The van was well equipped, with a full-size oven and a microwave. He reached for his wallet. Cooking was definitely not part of his holiday plans. It had been dark last night when he'd arrived, but he'd thought he'd seen a pizza takeaway just before he'd turned into the site. That would be a good place to start.

Half an hour later, armed with a pizza the size of his laptop computer and a bottle of red wine from the off-licence to go with it, he let himself back into the caravan. A quick search of the cupboards and drawers yielded plates, cutlery and glasses, but no corkscrew. Neither had he thought to bring one with him. Perhaps they'd have one in the site shop, if it was still open. He was just pondering on whether he could be bothered to go and ask when there was a hesitant knock at the door.

Frowning, he went to answer it. When he swung it open, he found himself face to face with the woman from the beach.

'Amy tells me your name is Tom and that she saw you coming in here a few moments ago,' she said.

'Amy's very observant,' he said, noticing with relief that she didn't look drunk any more, although she did look a bit uncomfortable. He waited for her to continue.

'I just popped over to say thank you for bringing her back earlier — and to apologise. I must have seemed awfully rude.'

Politeness made him shake his head. 'Come in a minute.'

She stepped up into the doorway, noticed the pizza box on the table and said, 'Sorry, I'm interrupting your meal.'

'It'll stay warm for ages. I was just contemplating whether to go and get a corkscrew, so I could have a glass of wine with it. I didn't think to bring one with me.' He broke off, suddenly embarrassed, but all she said was, 'You can borrow mine if you like. I'll pop back and get it.'

'Don't worry,' he said, but she was already out of the door.

'What an idiot!' he thought, as he watched her go towards the caravan opposite his. She must have felt bad enough already without him blundering in. On the other hand, getting so drunk that you weren't keeping a proper eye on your child really wasn't on. Maybe it would be a good idea if he took charge of her corkscrew permanently.

A few minutes later he saw her hurrying back. She didn't attempt to come in, just handed him the corkscrew from the door.

'Give it back to me later. No rush.' Then she smiled and was gone again, before he could speak.

She was a very pretty woman to have a drink problem, he thought, as he opened the wine and cut the pizza into slices. Not that you could tell by appearances. Susannah had been a stunner when he met her. Still was, he thought ruefully, but it was strange — when you got to know someone, their personality overrode a lot of the physical stuff. For him, Susannah's beautiful face was marred by lines of discontent. He no longer saw the amazing blue of her eyes, just the frantic insecurity that glittered in them.

The only regret he didn't have about their marriage was Josh. An image of his son flicked into his mind. He'd inherited his mother's perfect bone structure and his father's dark hair and olive skin. As always, when he thought of his son, he felt a swell of emotion.

Josh had looked perfect from the day he was born. He still couldn't look at him without feeling an ache of love so intense that it hurt. Maybe that was the difference between love for someone who was fundamentally separate from you and love for someone you'd helped to create.

He ate the fourth slice of pizza and decided to keep the rest for lunch tomorrow. Then he re-corked the bottle of wine. He'd better take the corkscrew back. Keeping it was hardly going to make a difference anyway.

Amy opened the door to his hesitant knock. 'Hi, Tom,' she said, grinning at him. 'Mummy's in the loo. Come in,' she added, jumping up and down in her bare feet.

Hesitantly, he followed her into the van, which was a mirror image of his except that the seat covers were a deep orange instead of navy and there was a pile of magazines on the table. Not a wine bottle in sight, rather to his relief.

'Who is it, Amy?' called a muffled

voice from the direction of the bathroom.

'It's me — Tom. Just returning your corkscrew,' he called.

'I'll be right there.' Then he heard the bolt click back and she emerged. 'Thank you.' She took the corkscrew from his hands. 'I'm Rowena, by the way. Rowena Jackson.'

'Tom Lockey.'

'Well, now we've been properly introduced, maybe I can apologise for earlier.' Her dark eyes met his. 'I really didn't mean to fly at you like that. I hardly knew what I was saying.'

'Yes, I could see that,' he said gravely.

She pushed a hand through her long, dark hair. 'It doesn't happen very often, but now and then I'm not quite quick enough to catch it.' She glanced at him. 'It's a right pain being diabetic.'

'Oh, I see . . . Diabetic?'

She frowned. 'Yes. What did you think was happening?'

Involuntarily, he glanced at the corkscrew she was still holding and

Rowena burst into a peal of laughter. 'You thought I was drunk! No wonder you brought this back so quickly.' She laughed again and he could feel himself reddening. Then, as if suddenly aware of his discomfort, she said, 'I'm sorry. I'm not laughing at you. It's an easy mistake to make. Look, if you're not rushing off, let me make you a coffee.'

He was about to refuse but she put a hand on his arm. 'Please. It's the least I can do.'

'Sit here, Tom, sit here.' Amy patted the cushions on the bench seat by the window and reluctantly he went and sat beside her.

'This is Puff,' she said, showing him the toy she was holding. 'He's my dragon and I'm teaching him to fly.'

'Oh, right.' He glanced at the toy, which was pink with floppy ears and a spindly tail, and looked more like a mutant donkey than a dragon.

Amy grinned at him, her brown eyes sparkling, and he thought, 'I must be mad, sitting here, making small talk with somebody else's child when I should be with my own.'

'What's your little boy's name?' Amy asked, almost as if she was tuning into his thoughts. He glanced at her, startled.

'Amy thinks everyone's got children,' Rowena said, coming across to the table. Although she was smiling, she seemed tense.

'Well, she's right in my case. His name's Josh.' He glanced at Amy, only partly reassured by her mother's explanation. 'He's a bit older than you. He's nearly ten.'

'Is he with his mummy, then?'

'Yes.' He was beginning to feel uncomfortable. When she'd asked Josh's name, she hadn't talked as though she'd been guessing but as if she already knew he had a son. He struggled to remember if he'd mentioned Josh on the beach.

Before he could pursue this line of thought, Rowena put a mug of coffee on the table. 'Amy tells me you're an artist.'

He nodded, reluctant to discuss his

work. Most people thought it must be a fascinating job, involving exotic locations and scantily clad models, and were disillusioned when he told them he spent most of his time doing bread-and-butter stuff like pet portraits.

'I'm a yoga teacher,' she said. 'For adult education.'

It made sense, he thought, watching her go to get Amy's cup, complete with striped red straw, from the worktop. She was poised and controlled, which must make what had happened on the beach even harder for her.

'You didn't look at all well earlier.'

'I let my blood sugar drop too low. I'd realised and had a biscuit, but I was just a bit too late. I'm usually a lot more careful,' she went on, 'but what with being here and relaxing, I wasn't quite as vigilant as normal. It was a stupid thing to do.' Her face darkened and he felt compelled to say something to make her feel better.

'Don't be too hard on yourself. These things happen.'

She shook her head and looked at Amy. 'I'd never forgive myself if something happened to her just because I wasn't careful enough. Anyway . . . ' Her voice changed. 'I thought we were talking about you. So are you a professional artist? Or is it a hobby — an excuse to ogle all the pretty girls on the beach?'

'I'm a professional,' he said, stung.

She grinned. 'I'm teasing you.'

He smiled back, not sure if she was flirting with him or just being friendly. God, he was out of practice. He'd spent so many years having to be careful what he said around Susannah that he'd forgotten the art of banter. 'I'm supposed to be here with Josh,' he said. 'But he was ill at the last minute, so he stayed behind with his mother.'

'What a shame.'

'Susannah's going to bring him later in the week if he's better.' He stood up. 'Anyway, thanks for the coffee but I'd better get back.'

'Sure.' She smiled at him. 'We're here

on our own, too. So if you fancy some company on the beach tomorrow, give us a knock. I promise I won't snap your head off like I did this afternoon.'

'OK, thanks. Good night then, both of you.'

'Night, Tom.' Amy sucked air noisily from the bottom of her cup and stared at him over the top of it, her brown eyes huge.

As he pulled the door closed behind him, he felt a little twist in his gut. Alone or not, the last thing he wanted to do was spend time with a family that wasn't his. It would remind him all too painfully of what he no longer had. He headed back to his caravan, poured himself another glass of wine and wondered what had happened to Amy's father. Probably tucked away somewhere, a maintenance cheque his only link with his family, he thought, wondering when he'd become so cynical.

Remembering that he hadn't phoned Susannah, he tried her now, but the phone just rang and rang and eventually he hung up, with a frown. Josh obviously wasn't ill enough to stop her going out.

The next day he woke up early to a sky that was hazy with cloud. It was still muggy, though, and would probably be hot when the sun burnt through. He decided to head off with a rucksack and explore the nearest bit of the Dorset coast path. The curtains were still drawn in Rowena's caravan, he saw as he passed, which was just as well, as it meant he wouldn't need to make any excuses for not joining them.

He found a signpost and headed up the hillside on to the rocky cliff path at the top and soon he was alone, with just birdsong and the occasional sheep for company. He sucked the clear sea air into his lungs and realised he hadn't felt this free for a long time. By midday, the sky had cleared and was the same glittering blue as the sea, which lay in a curved basin at the foot of the sheer cliffs. The bottle of water he'd brought with him wasn't much of a match for the combination of steep hills and steadily growing heat, and he was relieved to come down yet another sheer path to find himself within spitting distance of a pub.

Fortified with a cheese ploughman's and half a pint of Guinness, he sat at a wooden table outside and tried to get hold of Susannah again. But the surrounding hills were obviously too much for the signal to get through, so in the end he went into the pub, only to find that there was no public phone.

'One up by the crossroads,' the landlord told him. 'That's if it's working. You can use ours if it's urgent.'

'No, it's all right.' Tom gestured to his mobile. 'I'll probably get a signal when I get up top again.'

In the end, he didn't get round to phoning Susannah because the view from the next hill was so breathtaking. The only thought in his mind was that he should have brought some form of capturing it. A sketchpad wouldn't have been much good. You needed colour to do justice to the sweep of pink heather dipping to sandstone cliffs that gleamed gold beneath the sun. One of those perfect summer days that were so rare in England, incomparable to anywhere abroad he'd ever been.

Even the colours in the sea were spectacular. A mix of turquoise and silver that stretched back towards the cliffs, sometimes breaking in sheets of white spray over the surrounding rocks, sometimes lapping in creamy breakers on the shore. He wasn't sure he could have done it justice even if he'd had the means to paint it.

Glad of the decent walking boots he'd splashed out on, he walked all day. By the time the holiday park was back in sight again, the sun was like a great orange as it sank into a flame-streaked horizon. Staying out all day had cleared his head. He'd get back, phone Susannah and they could sort something out for the rest of the week. The sea air would do Josh good.

He was just nearing the bit of cliff

path that dropped back down to the holiday park when he spotted something pink lying in the long grass alongside the path. He bent, curious, and saw that it was a child's toy. Puff, he realised, as he picked it up. Amy must have dropped him. He'd pop in on the way back and reunite them.

Rowena answered the door to his knock. 'Oh thank you so much,' she said. 'We've been looking for him for the past hour. Amy, look who's turned up,' she called over her shoulder. 'Puff's back.'

He saw the little girl's face light up as she came to stand beside her.

'All safe and sound,' he said, handing him to her.

Rowena smiled. 'What do you say to Tom?'

'Thank you,' Amy whispered, hugging the toy.

'My pleasure.' He was about to turn to go back to his van when Rowena said impulsively, 'Will you join us for tea tonight, Tom? We owe you one.'

He was about to refuse, but then it struck him that it was a much better idea than sitting alone in his caravan again. 'Yes, all right,' he said. 'What time shall come?'

'It'll take me about half an hour to knock up a gourmet feast. So any time you're ready after that.'

The gourmet feast turned out to be chicken, chips and salad, which they ate with the bottle of wine he'd brought with him, although Amy had beans instead of salad, and blackcurrant juice instead of wine. He found he was starting to relax a bit in their company.

Amy was bright and intuitive and full of questions. 'Can I play with Josh when he gets here?' she asked, when they'd eaten and were contemplating whether they could manage any more ice-cream.

'If he comes,' he said, glancing at her.

Amy smiled back at him and once again he had the impression of someone much older.

'There's no sign of them joining you

yet, then?' Rowena asked.

He shook his head. 'No, not yet.'

'Well, let's hope the weather holds out for when they do.'

He nodded and said no more, and she didn't push it. She stood up and started to gather their plates.

'How's Puff now?' he asked Amy, who had the toy on her lap and had been feeding him pretend chips throughout the meal.

'Puff's very tired,' she said. 'He doesn't want any more flying lessons. He doesn't mind about not flying, he said.'

'Not all dragons fly, you know. Some of them guard damsels.'

'What's a damsel?'

'A very pretty lady,' he said. 'Just like you.'

Amy giggled, and Tom became aware that Rowena was watching him, a softness in her eyes. He shut up, feeling awkward as she came back to the table.

'I think it's about time that damsels and dragons were in bed,' she said, and smiled at Tom.

'My cue to go.'

'I haven't made you coffee yet.'

'I'll do it while you're putting her to bed.'

'All right. Thanks.'

They disappeared into the back of the van. He got up and put the kettle on and spooned coffee into mugs. He was just adding hot water when his mobile rang. Susannah, he saw, as the number flashed up on the display. About time too.

'Hi,' he said, 'I've been trying to get hold of you.'

'Is Josh with you?' she said without preamble.

'No, of course he's not with me.' His head spun in a little burst of shock. 'Why should he be? You've got him.'

'No I haven't . . . ' She started to sob.

Horrified, he tried to keep the panic from his voice. 'Susannah, just calm down and tell me what's happened.' He could hear her taking deep, ragged breaths and he forced himself to wait, to keep calm.

'We're at Mum's. We . . . came . . . earlier.' She gulped. 'Josh brought his bicycle — we were coming to you. He's been feeling better. But I wanted to see Mum. So we stopped on the way.'

Resisting the urge to tell her she was making no sense, he said, 'And what happened then?'

'Me and Mum were having coffee in the kitchen and Josh was playing outside. And then, oh, Tom . . . When I went to tell him we were ready to go, he wasn't there. Neither was his bike.'

Tom could feel a numbness starting to spread through him. He swore and Susannah began to sob again. This was getting them nowhere.

Forcing control back into his voice, he said, 'Look, maybe he thought he'd just come the rest of the way by himself. It's not very far and he knows where the campsite is.'

The words sounded hollow and unlikely even to him. What he'd said was true, but there was a main road to cross and he couldn't think of any reason why Josh should just go off on his own. But if he hadn't left his gran's of his own accord . . . Tom shuddered. The alternative was unthinkable.

'Drive here,' he told Susannah. 'I'll work my way back towards your mum's on foot. More chance of seeing him. Have you phoned the police?'

'No,' she whispered.

'Then do that too. I'll see you shortly.'

He hung up. Rowena had just come back into the main part of the van and he realised that she must have heard the tail end of his conversation.

'Is everything all right?' she asked, her face anxious.

'No.' He explained as briefly as he could. 'Could you just keep an eye out for him? He's nearly ten. He's got a red bicycle.' He could hear his words catching in his throat.

'Of course,' she said. 'You go.'

And then he was out of the door and running across the campsite, dodging between the vans. Adrenalin pumped through him, heightening his senses so that the grass seemed greener, the evening sky bluer. But all he could think was that the world was a dangerous place for a nine-year-old alone on his bike. Roads and clifftops and strangers who might do him harm . . .

He kept picturing Josh's face. If anything happened to him . . . No, nothing would happen to him. He wouldn't let it. He glanced at his watch. There was just an hour until darkness. He had to find him before then.

2

'I can't sleep, Mummy.' Amy came out of her bedroom just as the van door slammed behind Tom. She held Puff across her chest, her face half hidden behind the pink toy.

'You're supposed to be in bed, young lady,' Rowena murmured.

'I can't sleep. I saw a boy crying.' Amy looked up and her eyes were half knowing, half dreamy. Rowena felt goose bumps rise along her arms.

'It was a bad dream, darling, that's all.'

Amy shook her head. 'It wasn't a dream. It was like before. He was sitting down and he had a black mark on his face. Just here.' She touched her cheekbone. 'Did I see Josh, Mummy?'

'I don't know, darling.' Rowena crouched down and put her arms around her daughter, her mind racing.

Yesterday, when she'd chided her for talking to strangers, Amy had said to her, 'It's all right. Tom's got a little boy.'

At first Rowena had thought Amy had seen the child, but once she'd realised she hadn't, her uneasiness had grown. It was partly why she'd invited Tom to dinner — to see if there was some logical explanation, any explanation other than the one she didn't want to accept. That Amy was seeing into the future again.

'What did the little boy look like?' she asked now.

'He's got black hair,' Amy said and she was no longer looking at her mother but into the distance. 'He's soaking wet. And he's frightened.' Her eyes filled with tears.

'That's enough now. Come here, love.' Rowena kept talking until she could see that Amy was listening to her, seeing her face and not some vision in her mind. Then she picked her up and carried her back to bed.

'How do you fancy a hot milky?' she

asked, sitting on the edge and smoothing down the duvet.

Amy had her thumb in her mouth now, but her eyes were peaceful. She nodded and Rowena got up. 'No more looking at things, OK?'

'OK.'

Sighing, Rowena went into the tiny kitchen and put some milk in the microwave to heat up. She brushed a hand through her hair and screwed up her face, wishing she knew what to do. After all, she could hardly run after Tom and say, 'By the way, my daughter has these visions. I think she knows where your son is.' It had been hard enough for her to accept, and she'd had the last four years to get used to it. Besides, Tom didn't strike her as being the type of man who'd be sympathetic to such things. He was too down-to-earth, too practical.

She stirred chocolate into the milk and took it into the bedroom. 'Would Puff like a drink?' she asked.

'Puff's got a magic drink,' Amy said.

'So he can rescue damsons.'

'Damsels,' Rowena corrected, smiling. Tom had made quite an impression on Amy.

She waited until Amy's eyes were closed and she was breathing peacefully, then went back into the main part of the van. She glanced at her watch. It was a quarter to nine and the light was beginning to fade from the sky. Tom hadn't been gone long, she told herself. Any minute now he'd come striding back across the site with Josh pedalling along behind him. Everything would be fine, and she and Amy could carry on with their holiday, Tom and his family could carry on with theirs and their paths need never cross again.

But if he didn't come back with Josh, she knew she'd have to make a decision. Either let Tom and Susannah try and find Josh on their own, or say something about Amy's gift and risk them ridiculing her daughter. Because people still found it hard to accept.

When she'd met Amy's dad, Paul,

she'd thought he was merely intuitive. Then one day, he'd confessed that his mother and his grandmother had both been clairvoyant.

'I seem to have it too. Does it change the way you feel about me?' he'd asked her, smiling, slightly embarrassed.

She'd looked into his dark, gypsy eyes and known that nothing would ever change the way she felt about him.

They'd married and soon afterwards they'd had Amy. From the moment she'd been born and stared up at her mother with Paul's dark eyes, Rowena had known whom she'd take after. But for a long while Amy had seemed like every other little girl, with no more than the average number of imaginary friends.

Paul had died in a road accident just before Amy's third birthday. It was only after she'd lost her father that Amy's genetic heritage began to show itself. Rowena had thought it was the shock of losing him. She'd had plenty of nightmares of her own, reliving Paul's death. But eventually she'd had to admit that Amy was having more than childish nightmares. The things she told her mother had an uncanny way of becoming reality.

Now she hugged her arms around herself and stared out into the dusk creeping across the park, praying that Amy's vision of Josh with a bruise on his face wouldn't come to pass.

* * *

Tom's legs were beginning to seize up, the after-effects of a day spent walking and, the last ten minutes or so, running uphill. By the time he reached the cliff path, his breath was coming in gasps. He'd be no good to Josh if he keeled over. Standing still for a moment, he looked around him. The cliff edge was to his left, the stubbly grass innocently dipping away to the sheer drop below. To his right, the land undulated into what eventually became woodland. The surroundings that earlier he'd thought were wildly beautiful now seemed dangerously inhospitable.

He had to think rationally about this. If Josh were cycling to the holiday park, he'd go the way he knew, which was along the road. He'd only cut in to the coast path when he saw the sign for the site. Then Tom remembered that there were two signs. One of them was next to a footpath sign, a short cut for walkers. Josh would see that one first.

With this in mind, he turned off the path and headed towards the woodland. As he walked, he shouted, 'Josh! Josh, mate, where are you?' He wondered if Susannah had called the police yet. If only she'd let Josh come with him as they'd planned, this wouldn't be happening. He should have been firmer, insisted that he wait behind until Josh was over his cold. That's if he'd ever had one.

Seagulls were dipping and calling in the pink sky as he turned into the woods. It was cooler beneath the trees, the heat fading out of the day fast. He hurried, breathing in the earthy scents of the forest, his feet making hardly any noise on the sandy path. In a minute he would see Josh cycling towards him. As he went round each curve in the path, hope rose, then fell again.

He dialled Susannah's mobile. 'Any news?'

'Not yet. Where are you?'

'I'm on a footpath I think he might have taken. It leads up to the road.'

'I'm almost at the site. Mum's with me.' Her voice broke. Tom felt a wrench of compassion.

'I'll find him,' he said. 'I promise you, I'll find him. Don't worry.'

How exactly he was going to do that he had no idea, but he carried on calling as he walked. What if he got to the end of the path and he hadn't found him? They'd have covered every bit of ground between Josh's gran's and the campsite. That's if they were right and he was on his way here. He supposed there was the faintest chance he might have gone somewhere else. Gone for a cycle about without realising what a fuss it would cause. But no, Josh wouldn't do that. He'd tell his mum if he was going off somewhere, surely?

Just as he was thinking this, Tom saw a bicycle lying at the side of the path ahead. He broke into a run. A red bicycle. Josh's bike. The front wheel was slightly bent, he saw as he got closer, and the tyre was flat. His heart began to thump so fast that he thought his chest would explode.

'Josh!' he screamed into the swiftly falling dusk. 'Josh, where are you?'

The quietness of the woodland echoed back at him. Not quite silence; several small rustlings, a breeze touching the tops of the trees. Was Josh out there somewhere, hurt and afraid? Had he fallen off his bike and crawled, disorientated, into the undergrowth?

'Josh,' he called again, softer now.

'It's OK, Dad, I'm here.'

He went still, not sure if he'd imagined the voice. He circled on the spot, glancing around him. There was no one on the path.

'Over here,' the voice called, and he saw a tangle of undergrowth moving. Then he saw the familiar outline of his boy. Waves of relief crashed through him and then Josh was in his arms and he was hugging him so hard that he cried out, 'Stop it, Dad. You're hurting me.'

'I'm sorry.' He forced himself to pull away, to look at his son's face. 'Where have you been? Your mother's worried sick.'

'I was on my way to see you.'

'But Mum was bringing you to me anyway,' Tom said, puzzled.

'I know, but we were a long time at Gran's and I was worried you were going to phone again and say you had more work to do and I couldn't come yet — so I thought I'd surprise you.'

There was a glitter of tears in Josh's eyes and Tom frowned. The implications of what he'd just heard spun round in his mind. 'I haven't got any work with me,' he said softly. 'What made you think that?'

Josh shrugged and stared at the ground.

This wasn't the time for an inquisition, Tom thought, getting out his phone and looking at the display. Anyway, there had to be a mistake. Susannah wouldn't have said Josh was ill and then told the boy his father was too busy to fetch him.

'Are you phoning Mum?'

'In a minute — the signal's a bit weak here.'

'She's going to kill me.'

'Of course she isn't going to kill you.'

'Yep, she is.' Josh blinked a couple of times.

Concerned, Tom looked at him. 'You shouldn't have cycled off on your own like that, but she'll just be relieved you're OK. Don't worry, mate.'

'I don't mean about that.' Josh hesitated. 'I mean the bit about you working. She told me not to say anything.'

Tom felt a little tug of pain inside

him. 'I won't say anything about that.'

'What — never?'

'Not if you don't want me to.'

'I've hurt my knee,' Josh went on matter-of-factly. He rolled up his trouser leg to reveal a scraped bit of skin that was already turning blue around the edges. 'I was looking for one of those leaves you wrap around to help the bruise come out. But I couldn't find one.'

'I wondered why you'd left your bike.'

'I crashed into that tree. I think I hit a fir cone.'

'Do you think you can walk?'

'Yeah,' Josh said and took a couple of experimental steps. 'It doesn't hurt much.'

'I think the best thing we can do is to go back up to the road, then I can phone up and organise a lift.'

'What about my bike?'

'I'll carry it. No problem.' He certainly wasn't going to be able to push it. The front wheel was more buckled than it looked.

They went slowly along the path and Tom looked at his mobile phone again. Still no signal. 'You're going to love the van we've got,' he told Josh.

'If Mum lets me stay now. Dad, I feel a bit sick. Can we stop a minute?'

'Course we can.'

* * *

About twenty minutes after Tom had gone, Rowena saw a car pull up behind Tom's and two women got out. The younger one, presumably, his ex-wife, was beautiful. She had white-blonde hair and the bone structure of a model but, as she went towards Tom's van, Rowena saw that her face was pale and tear-stained. Poor woman must be frantic, she thought, concern overriding her desire not to get involved. They probably didn't have the key to Tom's van. The least she could do was offer them coffee.

'Hi, Mrs Lockey?' She went out to

meet them. 'I'm Rowena, Tom's neighbour — he told me about your little boy going missing. I'm really sorry. Is there anything I can do?'

'Thanks, love.' The older woman hesitated. 'The office was closed when we came by but I think it would be best if I nipped back to see if the police are there yet. You wait here, Susannah, in case he turns up.'

'Would you like a coffee?' Rowena said, as Susannah entered the van.

Susannah shook her head, sat on the bench seat where Tom had sat half an hour previously and stared into space. Rowena prayed Amy would stay in bed and not wake up with any more visions of Josh filling her mind.

'I'm sure Tom'll soon find him,' she said. 'Try not to worry.'

Susannah looked at her with blank eyes. 'This wouldn't have happened if he'd let him come down earlier.' She twisted her hands in her lap. 'All he thinks about is his work. Josh was so looking forward to this holiday.'

Rowena frowned. She was sure Tom had said his son was ill, but it wasn't her business. All that mattered right now was trying to comfort Susannah.

'He'll turn up, don't worry,' she murmured, praying that she was right. It was completely dark outside now, but at least the sky was clear and there was a moon sailing between the stars.

'What does he look like, your boy?' she asked idly.

'Just like his father.' Susannah's voice was bitter as she reached into her bag and took out a photograph.

It was true, Rowena saw. The child had the same sloe eyes as Tom and the same dark hair and olive skin, but he had his mother's delicate bone structure. 'He's got your lovely cheekbones,' she said.

Unease was trickling through her. They weren't back yet. She tried to remember what else Amy had said. It was something about Josh being frightened and being wet, which might mean he was by the sea. Perhaps Tom wasn't even looking in the right place.

* * *

'How are you feeling, mate?' Tom asked.

'Better.' Josh turned towards his father. 'But I don't want to go back yet.'

'Then we'll stay here,' Tom said easily.

They were sitting on a lichen covered log in a clearing just off the path. Tom knew they ought to get back while it was still light enough to see where they were going, but he'd realised as soon as they'd sat down that this wasn't about Josh feeling sick. His son had wanted to talk about stuff that had been going on at home. It had been difficult to listen to. Susannah had cancelled a trip to a theme park earlier in the year because she'd suspected Josh was coming down with mumps. By the time she'd realised he was fine, it had been too late for them to go. She'd told Josh, though, that his father had been too busy to pick him up because he had an important commission.

The more he heard, the angrier Tom felt. All those times she'd let Josh think that he'd let him down. How could she have deliberately hurt their child? He'd had no idea that she hated him this much — and the worst of it was that he couldn't even defend himself. He couldn't sit here and tell Josh that his mother was a liar, a manipulator. That would only end up damaging him more.

'Things are going to be different now, Josh,' he said, hearing the huskiness in his voice. 'Whatever's happened before, it's all in the past, I promise you.'

'How do I know you're telling the truth?' Josh said, and his clear voice was level. There was no bitterness in it. No resentment. He was just asking a question of his father. Asking whether it would be all right this time, because it hadn't been before. It nearly broke Tom's heart.

'I love you, Josh,' he told him quietly. 'I love you more than anything on earth. I will never knowingly let you down again. I give you my word.'

'Mum's always saying she loves me,' Josh said, and now there was a small sigh in his voice. 'And she says Uncle Simon loves me too. And that we're all going to be a proper family again when we move in with him. But I don't see how we can be, because you're not going to be there, Dad.'

He looked at his father in the moonlight and, as the log rocked a little beneath them, Tom could feel something tearing in his chest. Something splintering and shattering. It had nothing to do with Susannah and Uncle Simon, who was her latest boyfriend, but everything to do with the look in his son's eyes. That pleading look. Tom knew, suddenly, that this was his last chance to make things right between him and Josh. That he had to do something. And that he had to do it now.

'I think we'd better get going,' he said, standing up. 'I can give you a piggyback if your leg's too sore.'

'I'm too old for piggybacks. I think it's all right now.'

'And you don't feel sick any more?'

'No.'

'I'd better call your mum.' He got the phone out of his pocket. Still no signal. He wondered how long it would be before people started looking for them. Maybe there were already police with tracker dogs searching the woods.

'I don't like Uncle Simon,' Josh said, as they reached the end of the path that led out of the woods.

'Why not?'

'He's old and he's got BO and he's allergic to Murphy.'

'I see,' Tom said, smiling despite himself. 'Well, he can't help being allergic to Murphy. Lots of people are allergic to cats.'

'He can help kicking him when he thinks no one's looking,' Josh said vehemently. 'Just because Murphy was sick over his coat. He didn't mean to be — it was just a fur ball.' He hesitated and added, 'Maybe me and Murphy could come and live with you, Dad. Could we?'

'That'd be fine by me, but I don't think your mother would agree.'

'I don't see why she'd mind.' Josh kicked at a piece of tufty grass. 'Then she and Uncle Simon could go off and be a family on their own. And no one would be lonely.'

Tom glanced at his face in the moonlight. It was pale, he saw, and there was a bruise starting to spread across one cheekbone. 'Did you do that when you crashed your bike?'

'Yeah.' Josh grinned. 'Is it going black? It doesn't hurt.'

Tom wished he could say the same. There were all sorts of hurts swirling about inside him. All he'd ever wanted was to be able to keep some kind of a relationship with his son. Two days a fortnight. It wasn't much to ask, but she wasn't even prepared to let him have that. He could almost have understood her bitterness if he'd been the one who'd ended the marriage, but it hadn't been him who'd wanted a divorce.

'What are you thinking, Dad?' Josh asked, his face bright in the light of the moon.

'Not much,' Tom said, giving him a quick smile and wondering what Susannah would say if he didn't arrive back at the van.

It would be wrong to keep Josh from her, he knew that. Just as she'd been wrong to try and keep Josh from him. He had a signal now — he could phone her, let her know Josh was safe. But he couldn't bring himself to dial the numbers. He didn't think he could bear to speak to her.

'I think we'll leave your bike here,' he murmured. 'We can pick it up in the morning.'

They pushed it behind a bush not far from the road, hiding it so it couldn't be seen from the path. 'It'll be safe there till we come back.'

Josh nodded and Tom was touched at his son's unquestioning acceptance that they'd ever find the bike again. After all that had happened, he still trusted him. He'd have to make sure he didn't let him down, he thought, swallowing back the unease he felt. He wanted to keep walking, him and Josh safe in the warm cloak of the night. His mobile rang and he answered it, knowing his voice was brittle with tiredness. Susannah's voice cut through to him, shrill and demanding.

'It's all right,' he said. 'I've found him. He's safe.'

'And you're coming back.' It was a demand, not a question and something snapped inside him.

'Not yet, no,' he heard himself saying. 'We've got some talking to do, so you're going to have to wait a while.'

'Bring him back now. Right this minute, do you hear me, Tom?'

He pressed the disconnect button and then the off switch and slipped the phone back into his pocket. He should have stood up to her long ago, he thought. Not given in to her emotional blackmail. He'd come so close to losing his son. Would probably have lost him if Susannah had got her own way. Now he knew that he couldn't just take him back and hand him over, because if he did nothing would change. He had to make Josh understand that, however things might look, he loved him, that he'd never do anything to hurt him. He was aware that their whole future might hang on these few hours.

He held out his hand. 'How about we don't go straight back to the van? How about we find somewhere else to spend the night?'

'In the woods?' Josh's eyes were round.

'Well, no, I was thinking more along the lines of a little bed and breakfast. We can get ourselves a hot drink and I can have a proper look at that knee of yours.'

'Yeah, cool.' Josh grinned and Tom felt the weight inside him lift a little.

He wasn't going to abduct him — of course he wasn't. He just wanted a few hours alone with his son. A few hours to talk. That wasn't so wrong, was it?

* * *

Rowena looked anxiously at Susannah, who was still staring at her mobile phone in disbelief. 'What's happened?'

'Tom's found him.' Susannah's voice was hard.

'But that's good news, isn't it?' Rowena had a horrible feeling of unease.

'He says he's not bringing him back.'

'I don't understand.'

Susannah stood up, paced across the van and stared out of the window. 'I don't know if he told you,' she said quletly, 'but we're separated. Tom's always been jealous because Josh lives with me and not him.' She turned and Rowena was shocked at the look on her face. 'I know Tom seems normal, but he's not all that stable.'

Rowena went across to her, seriously worried now.

'Tom can be violent,' Susannah went on. 'He has terrible mood swings.'

Horrified, Rowena stared at her. Tom hadn't come across as unstable, but Amy's words about Josh were thundering in her mind: 'He's wet, Mummy, and he has a black mark on his face.'

'I'm scared,' said Susannah. 'Scared for Josh.'

3

Rowena had a sick feeling in her stomach. She'd been spared any more of Susannah's revelations about Tom and his violent mood swings when Susannah's mother had knocked on the van door and said the police were waiting to talk to them in the site office.

Once the two women had disappeared, Rowena sat with her head in her hands, snapshots of the last twenty-four hours flashing through her mind. Tom eating tea with them earlier this evening. His banter with Amy about dragons and damsels. Tom bringing Amy back to her yesterday on the beach. She remembered the look he'd given her when he'd mistaken the symptoms of a diabetic hypo for those of being inebriated, that accusatory look that you'd give to an irresponsible parent. Yet if what Susannah had just told her was true — and why shouldn't it be? — then it was Tom who was the irresponsible parent. No, worse than irresponsible. What kind of father would hurt his own child?

Something was niggling at the back of her mind, though. Something that didn't quite add up. If Tom really was violent, it seemed odd that Susannah had agreed Josh could come on holiday with his dad in the first place. Odd, too, that she'd sent him out to look for Josh when she'd just admitted she was scared he'd hurt him. But then there was Amy's vision of an injured and frightened Josh.

Frowning, Rowena got up and paced around the van. Tom had seemed so genuine. She'd liked him and even thought he was quite fanciable, she remembered with a little shudder. But then maybe that was because he had a look of Paul about him. They were both dark. They both had the same kind eyes. She swallowed.

The sound of the bedroom door

opening interrupted her thoughts and Amy appeared, her hair tangled, her small face flushed.

Rowena went to her. 'I'm sorry, darling. We didn't mean to wake you up.'

'Was that lady Josh's mummy?'

'That's right.'

'I don't like her.' Amy put her thumb in her mouth, something she rarely did these days, and looked at the floor.

Rowena knelt beside her. 'She's very worried about Josh,' she said gently. 'She's upset.' She put her hands on Amy's shoulders and, hating herself for disturbing her daughter's mind but having to know, she said, 'Have you seen him again, Amy? In that special place in your head?'

Amy nodded slowly. 'He's frightened of a nasty man.'

'Tom?' Rowena asked, closing her eyes.

'No! Not Tom.' Amy's voice was shrill. 'Not Tom. Not Tom!'

'All right, all right. I'm sorry. Look,

come and sit with me a minute. We'll get Puff.'

They sat by the window, Amy cuddling the pink dragon and Rowena cuddling her and wishing they were anywhere but here. Maybe tomorrow they could pack up and go home, pretend all this had never begun. It would depend on what happened, she decided. The last thing she wanted was for Amy to carry the nightmares with her.

There was a soft knock on the door and she opened it to let Susannah and her mother in again.

'They're going to start searching the woods,' Susannah said.

'Are you OK?' Rowena touched her arm and she nodded.

'I'll feel better when they've caught up with them, but they can't have got very far on foot. One of the officers is going to stay here in case they come back in the night. If Tom's planning on stealing my child, then he's going to need his car.'

Rowena could hear the bitterness in her voice, but she supposed you could hardly blame her for that. Involuntarily, she glanced at Amy, who was sitting, knees up to her chest, still hugging Puff.

Susannah, who was standing in front of her mother, followed her gaze. 'Your little girl?' she asked, her voice softening.

'Yes, this is Amy.'

'Hello, sweetheart.'

Amy didn't respond. She didn't even look up.

'Say hello, darling.' Rowena turned back to Susannah. 'Look, if you'd both like to stay here the night, you'd be very welcome. There's plenty of room. Or would you be happier out searching with the police?'

'No, I'll go back to Mum's, I think.' Susannah yawned. 'The police know what they're doing. But thanks for the offer. And thanks for the moral support.'

Behind her, her mother smiled. 'Yes,

thanks, love. You've been very kind.' Her face was softer than Susannah's but just as worried, Rowena thought.

They were just turning to leave when Amy said, quietly but distinctly, 'I saw Josh.'

Rowena felt herself go still inside, and Susannah's expression changed from disinterest to sharpness.

'You saw my son?' She looked quizzically at Amy.

'She didn't,' Rowena interrupted. 'Well, what I mean is that she didn't see him for real . . . ' She took a deep breath. 'I know this is going to be hard to take, but Amy sees things in her mind. Earlier this evening, she thought she saw Josh. You see, she's clairvoyant.'

'Is that right?' Susannah, not sounding at all surprised went across and sat on the settee beside Amy. 'So where did you see him, then?'

Amy sucked her thumb harder and didn't answer.

Rowena went and sat beside her. 'You can tell Susannah, love. It might help her to find him.’

‘Puff’s looking after him,’ Amy said and buried her face in the dragon’s soft body.

‘And this is Puff, is it?’ Susannah reached out her hand for the toy and Amy hugged him tighter.

‘He’s looking after Josh,’ she said again.

‘But he’s with you,’ Susannah pointed out, ‘so he can’t be with Josh as well as you.’

‘Puff’s magic. He can be anywhere he wants.’

Susannah shook her head, a frown creasing her forehead. ‘You’ve lost me,’ she said, glancing away from Amy and out of the window. ‘Oh well. I don’t suppose the police would take much notice of a child’s imagination anyway.’ Her voice was disparaging and Rowena wished Amy had never said anything.

‘You’re probably right,’ she said levelly. ‘Well, I do hope they find him soon. You’ll let me know, won’t you?’

‘Does Amy often have visions of

people she doesn't know?' Susannah's mother asked. She was looking at Rowena, her face kind.

'Not that often,' Rowena said cautiously.

'It's just that I know a bit about clairvoyance. Children are often particularly good at it, before we swamp them with our more traditional views of the world.' She looked as though she was about to say something else, but before she could speak, Susannah said, 'Oh come on, Mum, I'm exhausted Let's go back to yours.'

She all but dragged her mother out of the van. Susannah didn't look worried any more, Rowena though. Odd that, considering what she'd said about Tom being violent Something definitely wasn't right here, if it were Amy who was missing, she wouldn't be going home to bed, however exhausted she was. She'd be out searching high and low alongside the police.

* * *

It was after ten when Tom and Josh reached The Lighthouse Hotel, which had a 'vacancies' sign in the window and fairy lights on in the porch. The front door was locked, so Tom rang the bell and they waited on the doorstep.

'We'd like a twin room,' he said to the proprietor, who had a long, sombre face and a cheery voice.

'You're in luck. We've one left. I'll help you with your luggage.'

'No, I'll fetch it in a minute,' Tom said, averting his eyes and thinking how easy it was to lie. But it had been necessary, he thought, as he and Josh followed the man up a narrow, curving staircase. Admitting they didn't have luggage would surely arouse suspicion or perhaps he was just being paranoid because he was beginning to think he'd been a bit impulsive.

As the man unlocked a door and stood back for them to go ahead, Tom faltered. This was madness. He ought to take Joshua back to Susannah right now, before things got out of hand. He was about to say he'd changed his mind and that they wouldn't be wanting the room after all when Josh leapt ahead of him and bounced on the bed.

'This is cool, Dad. Can we get something to eat? I'm starving.'

'Can we?' Tom looked at the proprietor.

'Well, officially the kitchen's closed, but I expect I can knock you up a sandwich or something.'

'Thanks.' The door closed behind the proprietor and Tom sat beside Josh on the bed. 'This'll do us for tonight. We can go back to the van in the morning.'

'I think you ought to be getting our luggage in,' Josh said, with a sideways glance at him. 'Why did you say that, Dad, when it wasn't true?'

'I just thought it might look a bit odd that we'd turned up without any. Like we were up to no good or something.' Tom could feel himself reddening, but he was too tired to explain to Josh that some lies were all right, necessary even. Again, he felt his stomach lurch at what

Susannah was going to have to say about this when she caught up with him.

'But we're not up to no good, are we?' Josh said. 'I'm supposed to be on holiday with you this week. I think Mum's going to stay with Uncle Simon tomorrow anyway, so she won't mind.' He got off the bed and went and opened the bathroom door. 'There's a bath in here and a shower,' he called out, his voice echoing. He came out, fingering his cheekbone. 'I'm going to have a right black eye when this bruise comes out.'

'Yes, mate, you are.'

There was a knock on the door and Josh's sandwich arrived.

'When you've eaten that,' Tom said, 'run yourself a bath. How are you feeling? Are you tired?'

'Not really.'

Josh went back into the bathroom and a few moments later Tom heard him running the taps. He'd give him a minute, then he'd go in and they could have a proper chat, he thought, get a few things straightened out. But when he did rouse himself, he found Josh asleep in the bath, his feet tucked up around the taps. He stared down at his son, love catching in his throat. There was going to be no time for chatting tonight. The boy was exhausted.

He put the loo seat down and sat on it. Then he said softly, 'You shouldn't fall asleep in baths you know, you might drown.'

'I wasn't asleep,' Josh said sleepily. 'Just resting my eyes.'

He grinned and Tom handed him a towel. 'Your knee looks sore.'

'It's all right. I suppose my bike's a write-off, though.'

'It'll be fine. Just needs a new wheel.'

'Do you think Mum'll let me stay all week now?'

'I expect so,' Tom said, although he wasn't at all sure about that. Susannah was not going to be happy that he'd ignored her demand to bring Josh straight back. That didn't mean she'd take it out on Josh, though. He rubbed his temples and wished his head didn't ache so much. He still couldn't believe that she'd cancelled so many arrangements and told Josh that he'd been the one who'd changed the plans. Maybe tomorrow, when he'd talked to Josh some more, he'd find that there was some sort of mix-up. He hoped so. It was going to be tricky to find out without asking Susannah directly, and he'd promised Josh he wouldn't say anything. Things would be better after a good night's sleep; his head would be clearer then.

He left Josh to get dry and went and undressed for bed. It was wonderful having time alone with his son, but, deep down, he knew this wasn't the right way to go about it. All the same, he didn't regret bringing him here, he decided, as he switched on the bedside lamp and climbed into the single bed nearest the door. This was a time out of time and he'd face the consequences tomorrow.

In the morning, Tom awoke to the sound of rain drumming against the windows. He opened his eyes to see Josh padding about, already dressed.

'Fancy a cup of tea, Dad?'

'I can make it.'

'Already made.' He brought the cup and saucer across to him, the teabag string dangling out of it. 'I always make Mum and Uncle Simon one on Sundays.'

Tom felt a little wrench of pain. How easily this Uncle Simon had taken his place. 'Thanks, mate.' He sipped the tea. 'Doesn't sound like it's a very nice day out there.'

'It's not. Guess we're going to get wet on our way back.'

'We can always get a taxi.' By the time he'd paid the bill, he'd have just enough money for one.

'But then we won't be able to pick up my bike. I don't mind getting wet.'

'I expect it'll stop by the time we're ready to leave,' Tom said.

But it didn't. If anything, it got

worse, streaming down the hotel window beside their table as they ate sausage and beans followed by toast with jam from little packets.

'Can we still go walking on the coast path, Dad?'

'We can do whatever you like,' Tom said distractedly. 'We've plenty of wet weather gear. Pity it's all stuck in the van.' He'd been in that much of a hurry last night, he hadn't even stopped for a coat and Josh only had a light summer one.

Eventually they left the hotel just after ten, as the rain showed no sign of letting up.

'Right shiner of an eye you've got there,' the hotel proprietor said to Josh, as Tom paid him. 'Been fighting, have you?'

'Fell off my bike,' Josh said. 'Crashed it into a tree. We're just going to go and pick it up.'

'Are you now?' The man's voice was friendly, but he gave Josh a bit of an odd look. He was imagining things, Tom decided.

'We're going to have to make a run for it, Dad,' Josh called from the glass front door. 'It's pouring.'

'Come on, then.' Tom followed his son out into the rain and they ran up the road towards the woods.

'It'll be drier under the trees,' Josh shouted. Not that it made a lot of difference — they were both soaked by the time they got under cover.

'Maybe we should leave your bike,' Tom shouted, breathless. 'We can pick it up later in the car.'

'No, it's just in here.' Josh was running ahead of him, sliding over the wet leaves. At least his knee couldn't be hurting him much this morning, Tom thought, whose own legs felt decidedly stiff after all the walking he'd done the previous day.

They found the bike about ten minutes later, rather to Tom's surprise, and slowed to a walk through necessity. By the time they came out of the woods, the rain had eased into a fine mist of spray. When they got to the cliff path, he could see that the sun was breaking through milky-grey clouds across the sea and there was a bright, fresh smell of rain-washed grass in the air.

'Take it steady,' he called to Josh, as they came down the steeply curving cliff path. 'There's the holiday park, look, just on top of the cliffs.'

'Which van's ours?'

'You can't see it from here. It's at the front. There's a really good sea view, though.'

The rain stopped just as they reached the entrance of the site. A police car was parked up by the site office, Tom noticed uneasily. Must be a coincidence. By the time they were in view of his van, he was beginning to breathe normally again. There was no sign of a furious Susannah — no sign of anyone, in fact.

He was just fishing in his pocket for the key when a voice called out to him, 'Excuse me, sir, we'd like a word, if we may.'

He turned, his heart going nineteen to the dozen, to see two police officers, a man and a woman, walking towards them.

'Tom Lockey?' the man said pleasantly. 'And you must be Joshua?'

Josh nodded.

'Best you come with us, son.'

As Josh hesitated, Tom said, 'Go with you where? What's going on?'

Ignoring him, the policeman carried on addressing Josh. 'Your mother's very worried about you. We're going to take you to her now.'

'Over my dead body,' Tom said angrily, and Josh ducked away from the policeman's outstretched hand and quickly ran round to the other side of the van.

Time seemed to slow down and Tom was aware of several things at once. The policeman raced after Josh and the WPC began talking to him again.

'We just want a word, sir. Nothing to worry about.'

'You can't just take him.' He could

see Josh's frightened face through the windows of the van. 'For God's sake, you're scaring the life out of him.'

A flicker of movement caught his gaze and in the van opposite he saw Amy's face pressed against the window. Then Rowena came up behind her and pulled the curtain across, blocking his view.

'Josh!' he shouted. 'It's OK, don't be scared. Everything's fine.'

'Just a word, sir.' The policewoman's voice was beginning to grate on him. 'Won't take a minute. If you'd just like to come along with us.'

The policeman was coming back with Josh, one hand on his arm.

'Do I have to go with them, Dad?' Josh's dark eyes were huge and Tom had an overwhelming desire to knock the policeman over, but rationality was edging through his anger. 'At least let him get some dry clothes on,' Tom said, feeling a crushing weight in his chest.

As he spoke, the policewoman bent and smiled at Josh. 'Nasty black eye you've got there. Been fighting, have we, love?'

'I fell off my bike.' Josh's face went beetroot. 'Dad'll tell you.'

'I'm sure he will. Don't worry we'll soon have everything sorted out.'

They thought he'd done it, Tom realised, awareness seeping through him, colder than the sodden clothes that clung to him. What on earth had Susannah said to them?

'It's OK, Josh,' he said, forcing reassurance into his voice. 'You go with the lady and we'll sort everything out later. It's going to be fine.'

Tom watched them get into an unmarked car. As it bumped away across the field, he could see Josh's face, pale and scared in the window. Anger burned coldly in him, as he turned back to the remaining policeman. 'Is it all right if I get changed first?' he asked. 'You can come in with me, if you like. Make sure I don't do a runner.'

'I'll do that,' the man replied without a flicker, and followed him into the van.

* * *

Amy was inconsolable. 'Nasty man's got Josh!' she shouted, over and over, and nothing Rowena said could calm her.

'They're not nasty men, they're policeman, darling,' she murmured. 'They're helping Josh, not hurting him.'

In the moments before she'd pulled the curtain across the window, she'd seen Josh's face, like one frame of a film where someone had pressed the pause button. A wet child with black hair and a bruise across his cheekbone. Was that what her daughter had seen yesterday? Was that how it worked? You just caught glimpses of events that had yet to be?

She shivered. They'd go home today, she decided. The holiday was spoilt and it looked as though they'd had the best of the weather anyway. She pulled back the curtains and saw that the van opposite was empty. So the police had taken Tom away. They must have believed what Susannah had told them.

Last night she'd laid in bed, her mind whirling, and just before she'd fallen asleep she'd reached the uneasy conclusion that Susannah had been lying about Tom. But, unfair as that was and much as she liked him, it wasn't her problem. Amy was her responsibility and Amy had been upset enough over all this. She wanted to take her home, keep her safe, and she didn't want to bump into Tom again. Didn't want Amy involved with this family and their problems. The uneasy feeling that they were already involved, that it might not be as simple as that, nagged at the back of her mind, but she pushed it firmly away.

* * *

Tom sat in a bare little interview room that felt almost as cold as he was. It was bad enough that Susannah had lied to Josh, but to have told the police he was violent and that he'd abducted his own son was totally unbelievable.

'I was supposed to be on holiday with Josh this week,' he repeated, once more, 'so I'd have absolutely no reason to abduct him.'

'Funny sort of holiday, staying out all night in the rain.'

'We weren't out all night. We stayed in a bed and breakfast place. I told you.'

'But why would you want to stay in bed and breakfast when you had a perfectly good caravan to sleep in?'

'Susannah knew that I was bringing Josh back,' he said. 'We spoke on the phone last night and I told her.'

'According to her, you phoned her last night and told her that you weren't bringing Josh back.'

Tom gave up. 'Are you charging me with something? Have I done something wrong?'

'No one's charging you with anything, sir. As we've said, we just want to clear things up. We wouldn't be doing our job properly if we ignored calls about missing children and abductions.'

They finally said he could go and he walked back from the police station to the holiday park. It was still raining and by the time he got back he was wet through again.

A young girl was just going into Rowena's van with a box of cleaning stuff. They must have gone home. Strange — he was sure she'd said they were staying another week.

As soon as he got inside he picked up his mobile, which he'd left on the seat, and phoned Susannah. 'I've just spent the last hour being quizzed by the police,' he said. 'What the hell's going on?'

'You should have brought him straight back,' she said, her voice icy. 'You shouldn't have stolen my son from me.'

'I didn't steal him. Is he there? Can I talk to him?'

'He doesn't want to speak to you.' Her voice was rising. 'He never wants to speak to you again and neither do I.'

'Susannah, calm down. This is ridiculous! Josh is my son too. You can't stop me seeing him.' It took him a second or so to realise that he was talking to a dead line. She'd hung up on him.

Knowing it would be pointless to phone her back when she was in this sort of mood, he sat on the bench seat and rested his head in his hands. He'd been looking forward to this holiday for weeks. Looking forward to having some quality time with Josh, so that they could explore the coast path, swim in the sea, maybe go looking for fossils A precious week in which they could catch up, do the father and son stuff that he missed so much since he and Susannah had divorced. He looked out of the window at the rain slanting across the park. How on earth had it turned into this nightmare?

4

Three weeks later, on a beautiful, still day when the sea glittered and sparkled like a great plane of sapphires, Tom walked along the cliff top close to the caravan park where he'd holidayed with Josh. Or rather hadn't holidayed, he thought, with a twinge of pain. The memory of being questioned by the police still haunted him, but far worse was the fact that Susannah had refused to speak to him since that day, or to let him speak to Josh. He tortured himself with what she might be telling their son, but there was absolutely nothing he could do about it. Whenever he phoned, she hung up on him. In the end he'd driven round there, but she'd refused to speak to him, sending her boyfriend to the door instead.

Josh's description of 'Uncle Simon' hadn't been far off. He must have been in his mid forties, a good ten years older than Susannah, and he smelt not of BO as Josh had said, but of a rather pungent aftershave.

'I just want to see my son,' Tom had said, deciding that appealing to the man's better nature was probably his best bet. 'I have access arrangements and I'd like them honoured.'

He saw the hesitation in the man's face. Then he heard Susannah's voice in the background. 'Tell him to get lost, Si, will you? Josh doesn't want to see him anyway.'

He was tempted to refuse to leave until he'd spoken to her, but he didn't want to upset Josh, if he was there, by getting into an argument. Susannah, as usual, held all the cards. She knew that applying for a court order to enforce his access arrangements could take weeks.

He wasn't giving up, though. Today he'd decided to visit Susannah's mother, Connie. He'd phoned her earlier and she'd told him she didn't want to get involved, that it was between him and

Susannah. So he'd driven the thirty miles here instead. Connie wasn't unreasonable. If he could persuade her to listen to him for five minutes, he was sure he could convince her to talk some sense into her daughter.

Now he was walking on the cliffs near her house, trying to decide how best to get her to listen to him. If she closed the door in his face, he'd have wasted his time. He still hadn't decided on a plan of action when he heard his name being called. It was a child's voice and hope leapt inside him. Josh? Except it wasn't Josh who was running along the cliff path towards him. It was Amy.

'Hello there,' he said, as she reached his side, her toy dragon Puff clutched in her hands.

'Hi, Tom,' she said, grinning and not looking a bit surprised to see him.

Rowena caught up with her daughter and Tom smiled at her, unsure of his reception. He wasn't sure if they'd cut short their holiday because of something Susannah had said about him. 'So are you back on holiday again?' he said. 'Or is this just a coincidence?'

'A coincidence.' Rowena glanced at her daughter wryly. 'Amy nagged and nagged me to bring her here today. Are you here with Josh?'

'No, I'm not.' He paused and then decided to plunge in and tell her what had happened. 'Susannah's stopped me from seeing him,' he finished. 'She told the police I'd abducted him — among other things.' Rowena blushed, and he said, 'She told you too, eh? So did you believe her? Did you think I might hurt Josh?'

For a moment she was silent and while he waited for her answer he was acutely aware of the fresh sea breeze that lifted her dark hair, and the call of the gulls and the swish of distant waves on the beach below.

Then she shook her head and met his eyes. 'No,' she said quietly. 'I was a bit taken aback at first. She seemed so genuine and she was so upset, but then when I thought about it, I realised it didn't make any sense. After all, I'd heard her phone you and ask for your help. I knew she wouldn't have done that if she was really worried.'

'I thought your sudden departure might have been connected.'

'No — well, not directly. The weather had changed and Amy was a bit anxious about something.'

She bit her lip and he knew she wasn't telling him the truth. But then there was no reason why she should, he thought ruefully. They were virtual strangers whose paths had fleetingly crossed. It had hardly been in the best of circumstances.

They fell into step along the path, Amy running ahead, and for a while they made small talk.

Tom formed an idea. 'Rowena, would you do something for me?'

'What sort of something?' She looked startled.

'Would you go and see Susannah's mother and tell her about Susannah phoning and asking me to go out and look for Josh? She'd have no reason not to believe you.'

'But surely there's no reason why she shouldn't believe you, if you told her?'

'She won't believe me if Susannah's told her something else. I'm afraid she might not even let me in.' He touched her arm. She glanced at him and he could see she was still undecided. 'Please,' he said. 'I'm afraid I'm going to lose him if I don't sort something out soon. I'm running out of options. She only lives ten minutes away and it might make all the difference.'

'All right,' she said, at last, 'but don't get too hopeful. She might not let me in either.'

Half an hour later they were pulling up outside Susannah's mother's house. Rowena's stomach was churning at the prospect of having the door slammed in her face. The main reason she'd agreed to do this, she knew, was because she felt guilty that she'd ever believed Tom might be capable of hurting Josh. You only had to listen to the passion in his voice when he spoke about his son to know how he felt about him. But there was another, harder to acknowledge reason. She'd only come to this bit of the coast path today because Amy had begged her to. Had her daughter known they were going to bump into Tom? She certainly hadn't said anything, but then if she had, Rowena might not have brought her. Amy had been curiously quiet since they'd met him, her face serene.

'It's that house there,' Tom said, pointing. 'The one with the white gate. Number twenty-six.'

'OK. We won't be long.'

She and Amy walked up to the white gate and a moment later she was ringing the bell. All was quiet inside and then she saw a shadow coming towards the glass door and heard the chain being slid across.

'Hi,' she said, seeing the surprise on the older woman's face as the door opened a crack. 'I hope you don't mind me calling, but I was wondering if I could have a quick word?'

'Yes, yes of course.' Susannah's mother smiled as she recognised them. 'Come in a minute.' She undid the chain and led them through into a warm kitchen with pine cupboards and rows of herb pots lined up on the window-sill. The back door was open so you could see the neat garden outside. 'I'm just making some coffee, and I'm sure I can find some orange juice for your little girl — Amy, isn't it?'

Amy nodded shyly, glancing at the back door.

'She can go and play in the garden if she likes,' Susannah's mother said. 'I'm Connie, by the way. I don't think we've ever been properly introduced. We did appreciate your help over all that business with Josh,' she added.

'How is he now?' Rowena asked, glad they'd got on to the subject so easily. 'Not been giving you any more scares?'

'To be honest, I haven't seen a lot of him since then.' Connie's eyes were the same blue as her daughter's and they shadowed as she spoke. 'Susannah's scared to let him out of her sight. Can't blame her, I suppose.' She put a biscuit barrel on the table. 'Help yourself.'

'Thanks.' Rowena glanced out of the window.

'She'll be all right out there,' Connie said. 'I've locked the side gate since Josh's little expedition. She won't be able to reach the bolt.'

She turned back to the table and Rowena thought, 'It's now or never. I can't put off telling her why I'm here for much longer.' As she glanced around for inspiration, her gaze rested on a magazine on the table. She was amazed to see it was about psychic matters. Aware of Connie's eyes on her, she looked at her quizzically.

'It's an interest of mine,' Connie said in response. 'That's why I was intrigued when you mentioned that Amy had the gift.'

'Sometimes it feels more like a curse than a gift,' Rowena said.

'Oh, why's that?'

'It's upsetting for her.'

'You might find it's more upsetting for you than it is for Amy. She'll be used to it. It won't be frightening for her at all. It'll just be normal. Same as you or I looking out of the window and watching cars go by.'

'I'm not frightened of it,' Rowena said, wishing she hadn't started this conversation. 'I'd just like to know why she sees the things she does.'

Connie nodded and Rowena stared at a shaft of sunlight that fell across the wooden kitchen table, picking out the rich, warm tones in the wood. 'The thing I don't understand,' she went on quietly, 'is that it all seems so pointless. The visions Amy has don't seem to mean anything. She can't influence events in any way. She just sees them happening.'

'That's often the case when they're very young,' Connie said. 'Or when they haven't been taught how to deal with it. It's like anything in life — you may have a talent for something, but you still have to develop it. Learn how to control it, switch it off when necessary.'

Rowena sighed, glancing around the sunlit kitchen. 'I was rather hoping she'd grow out of it.'

'I doubt that she will. Not if she's having such strong clairvoyance at this age.' Connie hesitated. 'This sort of thing often runs in families, you know. Perhaps she inherited it from you.'

'No, she didn't.' Rowena was even more reluctant to pursue this avenue of conversation, but Connie's eyes were sympathetic and suddenly she felt compelled to unburden herself, talk to someone who wouldn't think she was nutty. 'She got it from her father. Paul was clairvoyant too. But we lost him when Amy was three. I wish he was still here. This would have all made sense to him.'

Connie leaned across the table and pressed her hand. 'Tell me,' she asked softly, 'what did Amy see the night Josh disappeared?'

'Not very much, to be honest. She just saw glimpses. That he had a bruise on his face, that he was wet and frightened. Later on she saw him struggling with what she called a nasty man. That was the bit that confused me. The other bit — well, I think I saw that too.'

'You had the same premonition as Amy?'

Rowena shook her head. 'No, I saw it for real. When Tom and Josh came back to the van, they were wet, soaked through. They'd been caught in a rainstorm. Amy was looking out of the window and she saw them. I pulled the curtain across but, just before I did it, I saw exactly what Amy had described. It was weird.' She hesitated. 'I don't know what she meant about the nasty man, though. She seemed to think it was the policeman. It didn't make sense.'

'Maybe Josh was frightened of the policeman,' Connie said, frowning. 'Amy wouldn't have known the difference. It sounds as though she has the type of premonitions where she actually feels what the person she's observing feels. So if Josh was frightened of the policeman, she'd have felt his fear. Does that make sense?'

'Yes, I suppose it does. You know quite a bit about it, don't you?'

'Only through reading and talks I've been to. I've never had the gift myself — not to any great degree. Although, saying that, we're all a bit psychic, you know. We've just forgotten how to use it.' She got up. 'Would you like another coffee?'

'No. No thanks, I'm fine.' Rowena smiled at her. 'I suppose I'd better tell you why I'm here.'

'I was wondering when you'd get around to it.' Connie's lips twitched. 'I assumed you didn't come round to talk psychic phenomena.'

Rowena smiled. 'No — although thinking about it, that's probably why we're here. Amy nagged me to come back. I cut short her holiday, you see, and I'd promised we'd come back when it was nicer. Anyway, she particularly wanted me to come today and we bumped into Tom on the cliffs. The more I think about it, the less it seems like a coincidence.'

'Then it probably wasn't,' Connie said, matter-of-factly. 'If you're anything like me, you don't believe in coincidence.' She glanced out of the window at Amy. 'Especially if you've got a psychic in the family. Did Tom ask you to come here?'

'Yes. He's missing Josh. I know it's not my business, but as fate — or whatever you want to call it — seems to keep throwing us together, I agreed to come. He seemed to think you might not let him in.'

'I told him I didn't want to get involved, but I wouldn't be so rude as to slam the door in his face.' Connie sighed. 'I expect he wants me to talk to Susannah, but it won't do any good. She's furious with him for disappearing with Josh like he did.'

Rowena nodded. 'I can understand

that, but I think he was pretty desperate. He said Susannah had stopped his access.' She let her words hang in the air.

Connie said, 'My daughter tells a different story. And he didn't help his case.'

'No.' Rowena paused. 'The police gave him quite a hard time about Josh's black eye.'

'He didn't do it. I know that.' Connie met her eyes. 'Susannah doesn't say these things to be malicious, though. It's not like that. It's never been like that with her.'

There was a small pause and Rowena felt embarrassed that she was having so frank a discussion with this woman she hardly knew.

Before she could speak, Connie said, 'My daughter suffers from depression. She's very bad at the moment. No one can get through to her when she's in this mood. She thinks the whole world's against her.' She got up and went across to the window and, after a moment's hesitation, Rowena joined her.

For a moment both women stared out into the garden. Amy was crouched by a flowerbed, engrossed in a butterfly that had settled on the buddleia. Rowena touched Connie's shoulder. It was odd, she thought. She'd built up a picture of Susannah as being a manipulative schemer who was determined to keep Josh from seeing his father, but now, standing here in Connie's kitchen, she was seeing a different picture. A troubled, insecure woman who was so afraid of losing her child that she was reluctant to let even his own father see him.

'Can't she get help — medical help, I mean?'

'She won't ask. She's terrified they'll take Josh from her, you see.'

'I can understand that. I'm diabetic.' Rowena told Connie about the day on the beach when she'd gone too long without food. 'When Tom brought Amy back, he thought I was drunk. You should have seen his face — so disapproving.' Both women smiled and Rowena went on, 'I know it's not the same thing, but not so long ago diabetes was a life-threatening disease. Today it's treatable, controllable. But so is depression. Susannah could get help if she asked. It's not so different.'

'You're very sensible,' Connie said, 'and I absolutely agree with you. But Susannah's very rigid. Everything's black and white with her. She can't bear to be out of control, admit there's a problem. She won't ask for help.' She glanced out of the window again. 'Your daughter has an ability that still isn't widely accepted today, even though it's New Age this, that and the other every time you open a magazine or newspaper. There's still a lot of prejudice. She's lucky to have you.'

Rowena smiled. 'I'm on a learning curve, but I guess that's part of being a parent.'

'Yes, it is.' They looked at each other and Connie said, 'Tell Tom not to worry. I'll speak to Susannah tonight and then I'll ring him. I didn't want to interfere, but perhaps on this occasion I should, for Josh's sake.'

'I'll tell him.'

Connie wrote something on a piece of paper. 'This is my phone number. Please keep in touch. And thanks for coming today — it couldn't have been easy.'

Her blue eyes were warm now and Rowena knew she was sincere. She called Amy in from the garden and they said their goodbyes. As they walked back towards Tom's car, she had a strong impression that she hadn't seen the last of Connie.

* * *

Tom, sitting in the car, glanced at his watch again and wondered for the umpteenth time what on earth they were doing in there. Asking Rowena to see Connie had seemed like a good idea earlier, but the longer he'd sat here, the more it had felt like cowardice, and he was cross with himself. He was never going to sort out his problems with Susannah by asking other people to intervene. Drumming his fingers on the steering wheel, he could feel his impatience growing into annoyance, and when finally he saw Amy and Rowena coming towards the car, the smile on Rowena's face did nothing to improve his mood.

He jumped out and went to meet them. 'I thought she must be cooking you dinner or something.'

'Sorry.' Rowena looked taken aback. 'We just got chatting. I didn't realise we'd been so long.'

'Is it OK for me to go in? What did she say about Josh?' He couldn't keep the irritation from his voice and Rowena touched his arm.

'Connie said she'll ring you later. She said not to worry.'

Irrational anger that they were on first-name terms rose in him. 'Great, so I just drive home and carry on waiting?'

'Tom! You asked me to go and see

her. Amy and I had actually planned a day on the beach.' Something in the sharpness of her voice cut through his mood.

'I know, I'm sorry. I'm just a bit uptight.' He pushed his hand through his hair, cursing himself for taking it out on the one person who was trying to help. 'Look, can I get you two lunch or something?'

'It might be better if you just took us back to my car,' Rowena said, 'I expect the ticket's run out by now. Then we can get on with our day and let you get on with yours.'

'Of course.' Chastened by her coolness, he drove them back, aware of the strained atmosphere in the car.

'Thanks,' she said, as they drew up beside her car.

'It's me who should be thanking you,' he said, anxious to restore the easiness that had existed between them. 'Are you sure you won't let me buy you lunch?'

'No, we're fine. But let me know how

you get on,' she said. 'And Tom — good luck.'

* * *

That night, unable to concentrate on the family portrait he was working on and too impatient to wait for Connie's call, he phoned her.

'I haven't been able to get hold of Susannah yet,' she told him. 'But I'll keep trying. Don't worry, Tom.'

Her voice was calm, reasonable, but he wished people would stop telling him not to worry. He went back to his easel. He was working from a photograph. Two blonde-haired children and their parents smiled into the camera, looking unrealistically happy. Banging down his paintbrush, he abandoned the idea of working and went into his garden. It was getting to that stage of summer when coolness closed in quickly once the heat of the day had gone. Breathing in the scents of dusk, he tried to force the image of Josh out of his mind and wished he had more patience.

Connie didn't phone back and he resisted the urge to phone her again. In the morning, he would go and see Susannah. Feeling better at the thought of doing something concrete, he cleared away his painting things and poured a drink. He was just settling down with the papers when the doorbell rang. Before he could answer, it rang again, 'OK, OK, I'm coming.' He pulled back the door, all set to give the caller a piece of his mind, and found that he was face to face with the last person on earth he'd expected to see: Susannah's boyfriend, Simon.

It didn't take a genius to work out that something was seriously wrong. The man's face was white and beaded with sweat. 'I'm sorry, but I had to come. Susannah's in hospital. I thought you should know.'

'What's happened? Has she had an accident? Where's Josh?'

'He's with a neighbour. I didn't know

what else to do with him. After the ambulance had gone, I came here.' His voice rose defensively.

Tom said, 'All right, don't worry. Just tell me what's happened.'

'They think she might have taken an overdose.'

Shocked, Tom stared at him, but it was obvious he wasn't going to get the full story out of Simon this minute. He looked pretty close to the edge himself.

Ten minutes later they were on their way to the hospital and Tom was still trying to piece together what had happened from Simon's garbled version of events. He and Susannah had rowed, it seemed, and they'd split up the previous day.

'I only went back because I had a phone call from Connie,' he told Tom, as he parked in the hospital car park 'She was worried because Susannah wasn't answering the phone, and I needed to pick up some of my things . . . ' He shrugged and didn't finish the sentence.

Tom, his anxiety increasing by the second, followed him into the hospital. They were shown into a side room and told by a young, serious faced doctor that Susannah had taken a massive overdose, that the drugs had caused her kidneys to fail and they should prepare themselves for the fact that she might not make it through the night.

Tom felt numbness creeping through him. 'Can we see her?'

'One at a time. She's in the intensive care unit.'

Tom let Simon go in first, waiting outside in the corridor. When the older man came out, his face was etched with pain. 'I'd no idea she would do this. I shouldn't have left her. She begged me not to go.'

'Don't beat yourself up over it.'

Tom went into the room. He wasn't sure what he'd expected, but it hadn't been this. Susannah's beautiful face was whiter than usual, but so peaceful. As if she simply slept. He'd come close to hating her these last few weeks, but he felt none of that now, just a deep sense of sadness as he looked down at her. What a terrible waste of a life.

He prayed that she would pull through — for Simon, hunched with grief out in the corridor, for Susannah, because he'd never dreamed she was as close to the edge as this. But most of all for their child — because if she didn't survive, how on earth was he going to find the words to tell Josh?

5

It felt strange having Josh around all the time — wonderful, but strange, Tom thought, as he made sausage and chips for the two of them. He'd often wished he could see more of Josh, but not in circumstances like these. Be careful what you wish for — wasn't that the saying? He carried the trays into the lounge, where Josh was sprawled on the settee, watching telly.

'Thanks, Dad. Have we got any ketchup left?'

'In the fridge.'

Josh went to get it and Tom sighed. He knew he should be grateful that Susannah hadn't died, but in some ways what she was going through now seemed even worse. Almost a fortnight had passed since she'd been rushed to hospital.

It had been such an enormous relief

when the doctors had told them that Susannah had survived the overdose and there would be no permanent damage — but the relief had been short-lived. She might have survived physically, but emotionally something had died in her.

Simon had warned him about it, but he'd still been shocked when he'd taken Josh in to visit and seen Susannah for himself.

'How you doing?' he'd murmured, plonking a bunch of grapes and her favourite magazine onto the bedside table.

She stared at him, her eyes blank, as if she didn't recognise who he was.

'Susannah, it's me, love — Tom.' He'd reached for her hand, but her fingers had felt limp in his, as unresponsive as her eyes. He'd wished fervently that he hadn't brought Josh.

Then she'd turned her head towards their son and he'd waited, impossible hope rising that it was just himself and Simon she'd cut off from.

'Hi, Mum,' Josh said, moving cautiously towards the bed. 'Brought your favourite toffees.' He put the paper bag into her hand and Tom held his breath. But Susannah just looked at Josh with the same bemused expression.

'It's all right, Mum,' Josh said, never taking his gaze from her face. 'You'll be better soon. The doctors will make you better.' Then he'd leaned forward and kissed Susannah's cheek.

Tom swallowed hard. Then Josh turned back to him and said, 'They will make her better, won't they, Dad?'

'Course they will.' He could hear the gruffness in his voice. 'It's just going to take a bit of time, that's all.'

He'd tried to talk to Josh about it when they got home. Explained that Susannah was very ill, but that the doctors were doing all they could to work out what was wrong.

'Is she hurting very much?' Josh had asked. 'She hasn't got anything in plaster.'

'She's hurting on the inside, where

it's not so easy to see,' Tom told him. 'Sometimes it's worse when it's on the inside. More difficult to diagnose.'

Josh had nodded thoughtfully. That evening he'd spent hours on Tom's laptop, connected to the Internet. When Tom went to see if he was all right, he'd explained that he was looking up Susannah's symptoms on a website he'd found.

'If there's anything you want to ask me, I'll do my best to answer it for you,' Tom said, kneeling beside him and wishing he didn't feel so helpless.

'How long will it be before Mum's better?' Josh had said, but that had been the only question that Tom couldn't answer.

Now, Josh came back into the room, ketchup bottle in hand. He squirted his dinner liberally and then said, with his mouth full, 'Good chips, Dad. You're getting better.'

Tom smiled at him. 'Glad you approve.' He was pretty sure that Susannah wouldn't approve of chips every night, but they were quick and Josh liked them, and it was hectic fitting in the hospital visits with his work and with looking after Josh. He told himself it wouldn't be for ever. They'd have more of a routine when Josh was back at school in two weeks' time. That's if he was still here then — and the way things were going, it looked as if he would be.

'Can we watch *Casualty*?' Josh asked, stretching to put his empty plate back on the coffee table.

'If we have to.' Tom had seen quite enough of hospitals without watching them on television too, but Josh had developed an overwhelming interest in anything medical. He supposed it was his way of dealing with it.

Tom washed up the dinner plates and went back to the lounge, but he couldn't concentrate on the TV. His mind was on his son. Josh seemed to have grown up this past fortnight, changed from a boy who knew roughly where the perimeters of his world lay into a young man who knew you could never take anything for granted. Not your father or your mother.

He was also worried about the future. He'd tried to explain to Susannah that he'd look after Josh for as long as she needed him to, but he wasn't even sure if she'd taken it in. She'd just nodded and waved him away. Simon was looking after Murphy, the cat, and he'd said he'd look after Susannah when she got out of hospital. Tom hoped it was more than guilt that was keeping him around.

He wished he shared Connie's confidence that things would turn out all right in the end. Once she'd got over the shock of what Susannah had tried to do, she'd been the one who'd seemed to accept the situation the most quickly. But then she'd always been down to earth.

'Things'll work out, you'll see.' They'd sat in the hospital canteen and she'd patted his hand. 'In some ways, this is a blessing in disguise. At least

Susannah's going to get the help she needs now.'

She looked at him, her blue eyes steady, and he'd felt uncomfortable. As if she was saying that in some way he'd been at fault because he hadn't realised how bad Susannah was.

'Don't blame yourself, Tom,' she said, reading his expression. 'I know it hasn't been easy for you these last few months. I think things will be better in future. I'll make sure she doesn't stop you seeing Josh again. He needs his dad.'

It was the closest she'd come to admitting he hadn't been entirely in the wrong when he'd run off with Josh. He knew loyalty to her daughter stopped her from saying more, but it was a good start. 'Thanks,' he said.

'Have you spoken to Rowena at all? Does she know about Susannah?'

He shook his head. He'd planned to. He felt a bit guilty, in fact, because of what had happened the last time they'd met. He'd asked for Rowena's help and then virtually thrown it back in her face. In normal circumstances, he'd have phoned up and apologised, but it had been the same day that Susannah had gone into hospital and that had wiped everything from his mind.

'I've got her number. I'll ring and let her know,' Connie had said.

'Thanks. I'll ring her at some point, too. I owe her an apology.'

He still hadn't phoned, though, and the longer it went on, the harder it became. Best to wait until Connie had explained about Susannah, he told himself, but deep down he thought he was probably kidding himself. Rowena was an attractive woman, who in another life he might have asked out for dinner. But his confidence around attractive women had taken a severe dent since Susannah.

'Josh, how do you fancy a trip to the beach at the weekend?' he asked his son, timing his question for when the credits were starting to roll. 'We never did get a proper holiday.'

'Sounds good,' Josh said, glancing at him. 'The weather's supposed to be nice on Saturday.'

'Saturday it is, then,' Tom said. Maybe between now and then he'd phone Rowena and ask her and Amy along. It would be good for Josh to have someone close to his own age to talk to. And it would kill two birds with one stone.

* * *

Amy, much to Rowena's relief, hadn't mentioned Tom or Josh since they'd bumped into them on the cliffs that day. There was a part of her that was surprised he hadn't been in touch. Maybe the situation hadn't improved, despite Connie's intervention. So much for fate taking a hand in things, she thought, going in to the kitchen to see how Amy was getting on with her painting.

'I'm doing a wedding,' Amy told her, flicking white paint across the table as she spoke, 'but you can't see the dress on white paper, so I'm doing it on black.'

'A bride in the dark, eh?' Rowena said, reaching for a piece of kitchen roll and mopping up the paint.

'No, Mummy, she's in a church and it hasn't got very big windows.'

'I see.'

The phone rang before either of them could say anything else and Rowena went to answer it.

'Hello, love, it's Connie.'

'Oh, hi, how are you? I was just wondering how Tom and Josh were getting on.'

'Well, I did tell you we're all a bit psychic.' Rowena could hear the smile in her voice. 'You must have tuned in. I'd have phoned you before but rather a lot's been going on.'

Rowena listened with growing concern as Connie told her about what had happened to Susannah.

'Simon found her just in time,' she finished. 'And I would never have phoned at all if you hadn't come round that day.'

'That was down to Tom. If he hadn't been so worried about Josh, he'd never have asked me to come.'

'But you only bumped into him because of Amy, didn't you?' Connie paused. 'I think we can safely say that my daughter is only alive because Amy persuaded you to take her to the coast that day.'

Rowena felt a shiver go through her. It would have sounded fantastic coming from anyone else, but said in Connie's quiet, rational voice, it seemed quite feasible. Whatever the reasons, Amy certainly seemed to have linked to the Lockey family.

'Are you still there?' Connie said.

'Yes. Sorry. I was just thinking about what you said the last time we met. About Amy's clairvoyance happening for a reason.'

'Probably best not to think about it too much.' Connie's voice softened. 'Sometimes all we can do is accept things at face value.'

They talked for a while longer about Tom and Josh, but Rowena still felt shaky when she put down the phone. It had been hard to accept that Amy did actually see things that were in the future. To accept that it was happening for a reason, far from being reassuring, was somehow even scarier. What if Amy was shown things that she could prevent and Rowena didn't interpret them quickly enough and because of it bad things happened? Did Amy even know what she was seeing?

When she finally plucked up the courage to phone Connie back and ask her advice, Connie said, 'The more we know about things, the less frightening they become. Learn as much as you can, but don't worry about it. You seem to be doing OK so far.' She hesitated, then added, 'I've quite a few books on clairvoyance. You can borrow them, if you like. Or if you just want to come over for a chat, you'd be more than welcome.'

A few days later, when Amy was at a friend's house for the morning, Rowena found herself doing just that it was a forty minute drive to Connie's, but the thought of sitting in her sunlit kitchen and being able to talk to someone who really understood her was too appealing to resist.

'So how's Susannah?' she asked.

'She's back at home now, although it will be a while before she has Josh back. He's with his dad.'

'That must be hard for her.'

Connie shook her head. 'I don't think she's really aware of what's going on at the moment. But she's going to be all right, that's the main thing.'

They spent a couple of hours chatting and by the time Rowena got up to go, she felt a lot better.

'Does Tom know about all this?' she asked idly, as Connie packed her up a box of books and magazines to take with her.

'He knows I'm interested in matters of a spiritual nature, if that's what you mean. But no, I haven't told him that Amy seems to have a hotline to the future where he and his family are concerned.'

Rowena smiled and said, 'I wouldn't have put him down as the type of man who'd take any of this seriously.'

'Oh, Tom's pretty open-minded. He's an artist,' Connie said, as if that explained everything. 'But I haven't told him about Amy because I rather thought I'd leave that up to you.'

'Me!' Rowena felt herself flushing. 'I don't suppose I'll ever see him again.'

'I wouldn't be too sure of that. Fate — or whatever you want to call it — has certainly made it her business to throw you together so far.' Connie hesitated and added, 'Right up to the divorce, I used to hope he and my daughter would get back together, for Josh's sake, but I've accepted now that they never will. At least now Tom will still be in Josh's life. Which is how it should be, if it's at all possible.' Her eyes were soft.

Rowena nodded. 'Amy was very

young when Paul died. She never talks about him, never asks questions.' She tucked a strand of hair behind her ear and said, 'I've often wondered if he might come back and see her. In spirit, I mean. Especially with Amy being the way she is. Is that possible, do you think?'

'It's possible, but I don't think real life is necessarily as pat as that.' Connie's voice was thoughtful. 'Sometimes you have to think a bit laterally about these things. He might still have a hand in your lives, you know, just indirectly. Nudging things in the right direction, so to speak.'

Rowena smiled. It was comforting to think Paul might still be around, looking out for them. She picked up the box of books. 'Thanks for these.'

'My pleasure. Keep them as long as you like. If you're worried about Amy at all, please don't hesitate to ring me. Any time.'

'I will.' Rowena took the box and Connie opened the door for her.

'Bye for now.'

As she drove home, she hoped Connie was right about Paul. Maybe it was down to him that they'd met Connie. Her own mother had died when she was small, as had Paul's, and they'd both been only children. It was one of the things they'd had in common, being independent. But lately it had felt more like loneliness than independence sometimes.

There'd been no man in her life since she'd lost Paul. He'd been her soul mate. It had been a once-in-a-lifetime kind of love and having experienced it, she didn't want to settle for anything less. But maybe she was wrong there, too. Maybe she should be more open-minded.

On her way back, she picked Amy up and they went into the house together. The light on the answer machine was flashing and Rowena played back the messages, realising with a jolt that one was from Tom.

'Hi, Rowena.' He sounded unsure of

himself. 'Just thought I'd give you a call. I understand Connie's told you what's happened. Heck, I hate talking to these things! Perhaps you could call me some time.'

She phoned him when Amy had gone to bed that evening.

'Thanks for calling back.' His voice was almost as hesitant as it had been on her machine. 'I meant to phone before, but it's been a bit hectic.'

'Yes,' she said. 'How's it going?'

He told her more or less what Connie had told her that morning. Then he added, 'Anyway, the reason I'm phoning is to say thanks. For going to see Connie for me that day. I was a bit offish with you, I know.'

'You were worried.'

'Yes, but that's no excuse.' He cleared his throat. 'Actually, I was wondering if you and Amy would like to come for a day out some time. Josh and I are going to the beach on Saturday. I know it's a bit short notice, but I thought you might like to join us. Then I could buy you lunch. By way of an apology.'

'You don't need to apologise.'

'I think I do. So, will you come?'

'Yes, we will,' she said impulsively. 'Amy would enjoy that, I'm sure. But don't worry about lunch. I'll bring a picnic.'

'Great. I'll look forward to it,' he said, warmth in his voice.

As she put down the phone, she realised that she was looking forward to it too.

* * *

Tom drove to Rowena's on Saturday, still unsure if this was a good idea. Guilt had prompted him to make the invitation. Guilt and Connie, who had encouraged him when he'd said he was thinking of it.

'It'll do you both good,' she'd said. He wasn't sure if she meant him and Josh, or him and Rowena, but he'd phoned and asked Rowena before he could change his mind.

Now they were on their way, the sun

warm on his face through the windscreen, and he was glad he'd asked her. Josh and Amy were sitting in the back, the picnic box between them, and it was good to hear them chatting. He had to admit that the prospect of spending the day in Rowena's company was appealing too.

They drove in companionable silence towards the coast and he parked in the same car park as he'd left her the last time they'd met. They walked down the cliff path to the beach, the children running ahead of them.

'Any news on Susannah?' Rowena asked, as they reached the sands, which were dotted with windshields and parasols and bright towels. The sea sparkled, rolling out to the horizon in a great stretch of blue.

'She's back home now,' Tom said. 'Simon, her boyfriend, is looking after her, and Connie pops in quite a bit, even though it's a trek from here.'

'She doesn't mind you having Josh, then?'

'No. I take him every couple of days and she seems quite happy with that. We haven't talked about what'll happen in the future, but I think it's going to be all right. I really do.'

'Good,' Rowena said, and he smiled at her.

Amy and Josh were up ahead of them. Amy was drawing something in the sand and Josh was looking at it, his head on one side.

'They're getting on well,' Tom said. 'Unusual that. Josh is usually quite shy with girls.'

'Amy's not a normal seven-year-old.'

Rowena's face was suddenly sombre and anxious to reassure her, he said, 'Is there any such thing as a normal seven-year-old? As a normal family, come to that?'

'I guess not. Looks like they've chosen where we're going to sit.'

They set out their towels and built a sandcastle close to the water, with a moat and tunnels so that the sea could fill it up. Then they paddled as they watched Amy and Josh playing chicken with the breakers. Tom could feel himself starting to relax. It was hard not to when the sun was high in the sky and the seawater was washing about your legs.

'Time for lunch,' Rowena said at twelve, and they went back and unwrapped sandwiches and crisps and bits of pork pie.

'This could give you food poisoning,' Josh said, peeling off the pastry and feeding the meat to a passing seagull.

'Josh!' Tom glanced at Rowena. 'I'm sorry. He's a bit absorbed with illnesses at the moment.'

'No, I'm not.' Josh glared at him, then flicked a glance at Amy. 'At least I don't go on about weddings all the time.'

'I don't go on about them,' Amy said, putting a bit of pork pie in her mouth and studying him. 'I just see them happening.'

'Don't talk with your mouth full,' Rowena said, feeling a shiver go through her even though the sun was still hot on her face.

Amy swallowed and said, 'I see lots of things, don't I, Mummy?'

'Yes, darling.'

'And today I saw a wedding. There were ever so many people and we were all dressed up and there were flowers everywhere.' She closed her eyes and sniffed the air, as if she could still smell them.

Rowena held her breath, aware that Tom was listening with interest Josh was listening too, his eyes narrowed into scepticism. 'I didn't see any wedding,' he said, scanning the beach as if he expected one to materialise. 'And I've been with you all morning.'

Amy opened her eyes and gave him a disdainful look 'It's not here, silly, it's in a church.' She put her head on one side and added thoughtfully, 'And we're all having strawberry ice-cream for afters, and champagne.'

'Yuck,' Josh said. 'I'm never getting married.'

'Yes you are,' Amy told him, her eyes serene. 'I might let you marry me one day.'

'No way.' He rolled over, kicking sand over her towel and she shrieked and reached for a handful to retaliate.

'If you two want an ice-cream, you'd better stop right there,' Tom said. He fished for some money in his pocket.

'Kids,' Rowena said, shaking her head, as they watched them running up the beach to the ice-cream van that was parked as far down the cliff path as it could get.

'So does Amy get her vivid imagination from her father or from you?'

'Oh, definitely her father. And it's not all in her imagination — but I think that bit was,' she added.

'How do you mean?'

'Well, I haven't been at many weddings where you get served strawberry ice-cream and champagne.'

'It sounds pretty good to me.' He paused. 'But that wasn't what I meant. You said it's not all in her imagination.'

'It's a long story.' She glanced at him and said, 'Sometimes Amy sees things that have yet to happen.'

He raised his eyebrows and she was suddenly scared he was going to mock her, but all he said was, 'You should talk to Connie some time. I mean, if you're serious. She's interested in clairvoyance and she's the most down-to-earth person I know.'

'I wouldn't have had you down as someone who'd be interested.'

'You don't know me very well,' Tom said. 'But who knows, if Amy's right and those two are going to get married, then we'll be seeing a lot more of each other. We'll have to, won't we — as parents of the happy couple?'

He grinned and lay back on his towel and she realised she'd been holding her breath. That his opinion, however lightly voiced, was important to her. She'd like to get to know him better too, she realised.

Around them, the sounds of the beach seemed to recede. Paul would never be far away, she thought, looking up into the infinite blueness of the sky. She sensed that he was with her on this one. It was time to look to the future, even if it wasn't as clear to her as it was to Amy.

'What are you thinking?' Tom asked, and she became aware that he was looking at her, his eyes questioning.

She propped herself onto one elbow and smiled at him. It could be fun going out with a man who couldn't read her mind. Different, but fun.

'I'll tell you sometime,' she said.

THE END